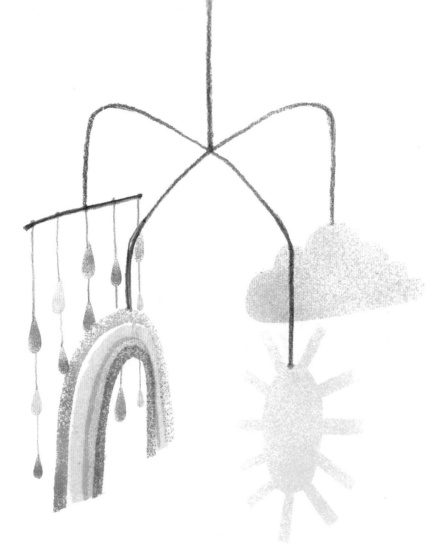

For information address HarperCollins Children's Books,

a division of HarperCollins Publishers, 195 Broadway, New York, NY 10007.

www.harpercollinschildrens.com

The artwork and hand-lettered text was created by hand-cut rubber stamps,

stencils, BLO pens, watercolors, and additional pencil line work, all composited digitally.

The text type is 23-point Abadi MT Light.

Library of Congress Cataloging-in-Publication Data

Names: Davis, Jacky, author. | Woodcock, Fiona, illustrator.

Title: Sunny-side up / by Jacky Davis ; illustrated by Fiona Woodcock.

Description: First edition. |

New York, NY : Greenwillow Books, an Imprint of HarperCollins Publishers, [2021] |

Audience: Ages 4–8. | Audience: Grades K–1. |

Summary: "A child uses her imagination to make the most of a dreary gray day"— Provided by publisher.

Identifiers: LCCN 2020037436 | ISBN 9780062573070 (hardcover)

Subjects: CYAC: Play—Fiction. | Imagination—Fiction. |

Fathers and daughters—Fiction. | Rain and rainfall—Fiction.

Classification: LCC PZ7.D288476 Sun 2021 | DDC [E]—dc23

LC record available at https://lccn.loc.gov/2020037436

First Edition

21 22 23 24 25 RTLO 10 9 8 7 6 5 4 3 2 1

GREENWILLOW BOOKS

SUNNY-SIDE UP

BY
Jacky Davis

ILLUSTRATED BY
Fiona Woodcock

GREENWILLOW BOOKS
An Imprint of HarperCollinsPublishers

Always for Sam—J. D.

For all the rainy-day den makers—F. W.

I choose.

I choose sunny-side up eggs
and toast
with butter, please.

Grape juice?
Yes!
Purple lips and happiness.

Pull open the shades

to let the sunshine in, and find

drips of gray sky covering everything.

What to do?

What to do on this rainy day?

Daddy says inside is where I have to stay.

I jump.

I jump up and down

and stomp my feet
on the ground.

I don't want to be
stuck inside all day.

I want to go
outside and play.

When the thunderclouds go *clap*,
Daddy pulls me to his lap.
He hugs me and holds me tight,
and says playing inside will be all right.

Okay,
okay, I say,
I will try to find fun
my way.
I run.

I run and slide, and dive into pillows where I hide.
In a soft nest filled with baby birds that I feed,
squiggly red and blue yarn worms is what they need.

I play.

I play with wooden blocks.

I build buildings really tall,

then bowl them over with a bouncy ball.

Blocks scatter and fall,

the ball bops down the hall.

And outside the rain won't stop.
I can hear it drip, drip, drop.

I duck.

I duck under the tablecloth.

It's my clubhouse,

where I draw and think.

I have paper, colored pencils, and a sippy drink.

I make.

I make make-believe muffins and pies.

Ones that you might like to try?

And outside the rain won't stop.
I can hear it drip, drip, drop.

Daddy says it's time for real food,

and then a nap.

I eat tomato soup and grilled cheese, okay.

But after lunch I will want to play.

I've had enough of this rainy day!

And by the way,

I howl and weep,
I won't.
I won't nap!

Daddy asks me to try,
try to use my words.

I finally say,
I will.
I will lie down
and not make a sound,
and listen to the falling rain.

And when I get up,
I paint lots of pictures
of clearing afternoon skies,
with yellow and blue birds
flying high.

And I read books,
and more books,
until Mommy comes home.

Then Mommy and I go for a walk.
We hold hands on the way to the park.
Sailing over puddles,

while the clouds move above our heads
and the sun peeks in and out.

Mommy pushes me on the swing
and we talk about our day.
And how badly I wanted to be outside to play.

Mommy says that she understands,
and reminds me that rain clouds *always* pass.

Then I skip and hop in the drying grass.

Spaghetti together,
plus a treat, yes, a treat for me.

I choose.
I choose strawberry ice cream,
with sprinkles, please.

And when it's time for bed,

two stories (and one more) are read.

Warm cinnamon milk and a kiss on my head.

I close.

I close my eyes,

and dream about my sunny day.

Where I found fun inside

when it was gray.